Happy Birthday, Spider McDrew

Collins
RED
STORYBOOK

Also by Alan Durant
Spider McDrew

Happy Birthday, Spider McDrew

Alan Durant

Illustrated by Martin Chatterton

Collins*Children's Books*
An imprint of HarperCollins*Publishers*

*For my daughter Amy and all her classmates at
Coombe Hill School, who made Wednesday
afternoons something to look forward to.*

First published in Great Britain by Collins in 1997
Collins is an imprint of HarperCollins *Publishers* Ltd
77-85 Fulham Palace Road, Hammersmith,
London, W6 8JB

3 5 7 9 8 6 4

Text copyright © Alan Durant 1997
Illustrations copyright © Martin Chatterton 1997

ISBN PB 0 00 675256 X

The author and illustrator assert the moral right to
be identified as the author and illustrator of the work.

Printed and bound in Great Britain by
Caledonian International Book Manufacturing Ltd,
Glasgow G64

Contents

Spider and the Doughnut Man

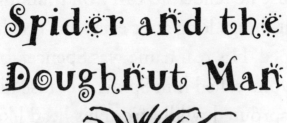

Spider McDrew was a hopeless case.
Everyone said so: his mum, his teacher
at Parkfield School, the other children in
his class. Sometimes they said it with a
sigh, sometimes they said it with a smile
and sometimes they said it with a heavy
groan. Mainly they said it when Spider got
things wrong – which he did quite often,

7

because he tended to carry on thinking about things long after everyone else had stopped. His real name was Spencer, but everyone called him Spider, because his hair sprouted wildly from his head like the leaves of a spider plant.

On this particular morning Spider McDrew was sitting at the back of the classroom, while Mr Smithers, his teacher, read a story about a baker and a little boy.

Spider wasn't actually listening to the story, he was studying the fingers of his right hand, which were stained with blue, red and purple ink from the felt-tipped pens he had been using. As ever, Spider looked the picture of mess: a splodge of blue ink smeared one cheek, the buttons of his cardigan were done up wrong and the bottom of his shirt hung out of his shorts like a large white tongue. He was also wearing one grey sock and one orange sock.

Mr Smithers finished the story. "Now," he said. "Who knows anything about baking?"

Hannah Stewart threw up her hand and Darren Kelly leapt into the air.

"Sit down please, Darren," said Mr Smithers.

"But sir, sir," Darren Kelly pleaded.

"Wait your turn," Mr Smithers told him. "Now, Hannah, what can you tell me?"

"My grandma bakes bread," Hannah said smugly. "It's the best bread in the whole world. My dad says so."

"Very good," said Mr Smithers. "And how does she bake it, do you know?"

Hannah Stewart pursed her lips and shook her head. "It's a secret," she said.

"Ah," said Mr Smithers. He turned towards Darren Kelly, who was reaching up so high with his hand that his face had gone purple. He was wriggling about on his chair too as if he needed to go to the toilet.

"OK, Darren. What can you tell us?" Mr Smithers asked.

There was an instant's pause while Darren Kelly caught his breath. Then, "I like cakes," he declared. He licked his lips. "Custard tarts, yum!"

"Jam doughnuts," said Kip Keen.

"Chocolate eclairs," said Neil Phillips.

All of a sudden, hands shot up like rockets around the room.

"OK, class, that will do," Mr Smithers said. "I asked who knows anything about baking, not what cakes you like. Now let's get back to the subject. Does anyone know anything about baking?"

For a moment all was still. Then an ink-smudged hand went up.

"Yes, Spider," said Mr Smithers.

"Why did the cream puff?" asked Spider

11

with a cheery grin. A murmur of puzzled amusement rippled round the class. Kip Keen nudged Jason Best who frowned and drilled his finger into the side of his head as if to suggest that Spider was totally mad.

"I beg your pardon, Spider," said Mr Smithers.

"Why did the cream puff?" Spider repeated happily. "It's a joke, sir," he added.

"Oh," said Mr Smithers. Darren Kelly jumped off his chair again.

"I know! I know!" he cried.

"When you sit down, Darren, you can tell us your answer," said Mr Smithers firmly. Darren Kelly did as he was told.

"Because it was tired out," he said.

Spider shook his head.

"Because it was a train," said Kip Keen. He pumped his arms, flicking off Hannah Stewart's hairband.

"Ow!" she shrieked.

"Puff puff, puff puff, puff puff, puff puff," went Kip Keen, his arms pumping faster now. "Whoo-ooo! Whoo-oo! Whoo–"

PEE-EEP!

Kip Keen's train impression was cut short by a loud blast of Mr Smithers' football whistle.

"Thank you, Kip," said Mr Smithers. "This is a classroom, not a railway track. Now, I think you'd better put us all out of our misery, Spider. Why *did* the cream puff?"

Everyone turned towards Spider to hear the answer. Spider looked at Mr Smithers. He opened his mouth. . . and his mind wandered.

"Gingerbread men," he said.

For a moment there was complete silence in the room. Then Jason Best groaned.

"That's not a joke," he grumbled. "It's not even funny. Why did the cream puff? Gingerbread men."

"It doesn't make sense," Neil Phillips agreed.

"It's cra-azy," Darren Kelly said, shaking his head wildly.

"I think you'd better explain the joke, Spider," sighed Mr Smithers.

But Spider couldn't explain. He couldn't say a word. He knew he'd made a mistake but his tongue was stuck as fast as if set in treacle. He wanted to say that gingerbread men were his favourite sort of cake, but his tongue would not move. He stared back helplessly at his teacher.

It was Emma Flowers who came to his rescue.

"I think Spider's got the joke wrong," she said matter-of-factly.

"Yes, I think perhaps he has," said Mr Smithers. "Can you tell us the answer then, Emma?"

"Yes, sir," she said. "It goes like this, yeah: why did the cream puff? Because it saw the apple turnover."

Nobody laughed, except Darren Kelly who cackled and fell off his chair.

"Darren!" said Mr Smithers sternly.

When everyone had settled down, Mr Smithers explained that a cream puff and

an apple turnover were both kinds of cake.
Then he looked at the class and smiled.

"Now, I've got something special to tell
you," he said. "On Friday we are going to
visit a bakery, so you'll all be able to see
for yourselves how bread and cakes are
made."

The news was met with loud approval.
There were oohs and ahs and someone
cried "Hooray!" Everyone was bubbling
to the brim with excitement – except
Spider. He was still thinking about
gingerbread men. He was thinking about
the way his mum made them with a kind
of metal man-shaped stencil
and the raisins she put in for
the eyes and the taste of the
left-over mixture that she
let him scrape from the
bowl. He was thinking about
how delicious it tasted. . .

16

On Friday morning Spider's class stayed in the playground when the rest of the school went inside. Mr Smithers took the register, then he lined up the children in pairs. Spider's partner was Jack Smith.

"This is going to be great, isn't it?" Jack Smith whispered.

Spider frowned. "Is it?" he said. He had forgotten all about the bakery visit.

"Right, class, off we go," said Mr Smithers.

"Where are we going?" Spider asked.

"To the bakery, of course," Jack Smith replied.

"Quiet back there!" said Mrs Russell with a little wobble of her head. She was their music teacher but today she was helping Mr Smithers.

When they arrived at the bakery, the children were met by a short, tubby man with a red face and a huge moustache like a hairy coat hanger. He wore white overalls and a round blue hat that looked about two sizes too small for him.

"Good morning, children," said the man. "My name is Mr Fabrizio and I am the master baker." He raised his bushy eyebrows and waggled his moustache.

"Come with me and I will show you the secrets of my bakery. You will see cakes and bread beyond your wildest dreams."

"My grandma makes her own bread," piped Hannah Stewart.

"My mum gets her bread from the freezer," said Kip Keen, which made Mr Fabrizio smile.

"I don't really like bread," said Darren Kelly. "I just like cakes."

Mr Fabrizio's smile grew broader. "Ah, you will like my bread," he said. "Come, I will show you where the baking is done."

As the children followed Mr Fabrizio, he explained that his bakery made cakes and bread for lots of shops. He pointed to a big delivery van which, at that very moment, was waiting to be loaded up with goods from the bakery. When everyone was inside the building, Mr Fabrizio stopped and raised his fleshy hand in the air. Then he lifted his nose too and sniffed deeply.

"Smell that smell," he said. "Is that not wonderful?"

The children sniffed and agreed that the smell was wonderful – well, all except Spider. He didn't sniff, because he was too busy watching Mr Fabrizio's moustache. It was so very thick he couldn't imagine how the baker could smell anything through it.

"Do you think Mr Fabrizio's moustache goes right up his nose?" he asked Jack Smith.

"Maybe," said Jack Smith. But he wasn't really interested in Mr Fabrizio's moustache. He sniffed the air again. "I hope they make jam tarts," he said. "I love jam tarts."

The bakery did indeed make jam tarts – and custard tarts and treacle tarts, apple turnovers, iced buns, chocolate shortbread, Danish pastries and all kinds of other delicious cakes, as well as bread of every shape and size. The master baker led the children on a small tour, explaining to them how all these things were made. The high point for Spider was when they passed a woman making gingerbread men. He stopped and stared, his eyes wide with excitement. In the end, Jack Smith had to pull him away.

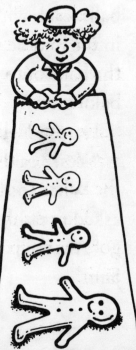

"Come on, Spider! We've got to move on," he said.

At the end of the tour, Mr Fabrizio gathered the children around him.

"Right," he said. "Now, I want you to watch very closely." He raised his eyebrows dramatically. "We are going to make doughnuts."

"Oooh," said the children happily. They looked on eagerly as the master baker shaped the doughnut mixture into small balls, each with a hollow in the middle. He put the balls onto a large baking tray.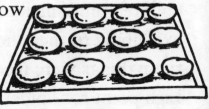

Darren Kelly shot up his hand.

"Yes?" said Mr Fabrizio.

"What about the jam?" Darren Kelly asked breathlessly. "Don't forget the jam."

"Ah, the jam," said Mr Fabrizio. "The jam."

He told the class that the choice of jam was very important. A doughnut could be spoilt if you used the wrong jam. The jam must be good jam, he said, this was the secret! He picked up the baking tray and carried it over to a big metal table.

"Now," he said, "I need a volunteer." At once a host of hands waved in the air.

"Me! Me!" pleaded a choir of voices. Mr Fabrizio stroked his moustache thoughtfully as he looked around the children. Then his gaze fell on a figure at the back of the group, the only one whose hand was not raised, the only one looking in the opposite direction.

"You, at the back," said Mr Fabrizio. "I choose you."

All the children turned. Then groaned. Spider McDrew said nothing. He continued to stare at the woman on the other side of the room who was making gingerbread men.

"Spider! Spider McDrew!" called Mrs Russell and she clapped her hands. "Come along now! Hurry up!"

Spider McDrew turned round, his face blank as flour.

"Mr Fabrizio needs your help," Mr Smithers explained.

"Oh," said Spider. Then, slowly, he moved forward.

"Right, Spider," said Mr Fabrizio. "You have a very, very important job. You are going to operate the jam squirter." He pointed at a machine on the big table: a large metal container

with a tube, on the end of which was a
nozzle.

"Now when I say 'press', you press this
button here," Mr Fabrizio said. "Like
this." He pressed the button and a blob of
jam dropped out of the nozzle into the
hollowed middle of one of the doughnuts.
"There," he said. "Easy. Can you do that?"

Spider smiled and nodded. "Yes, sir," he
said.

Mr Fabrizio picked up the baking tray
again. He held it under the nozzle.

"OK, press!" he commanded. Spider
pressed and another blob of jam landed in
the centre of a doughnut.

"Excellent," said Mr Fabrizio, moving
the tray slightly.

"Press!" he ordered again. Spider

pressed and as before the jam fell neatly into the hollow in the doughnut.

Soon all of the doughnuts were filled with jam. Mr Fabrizio picked up the tray to show the children.

"Yum," said Darren Kelly. "Can I try one?"

"They're not cooked yet!" Mr Fabrizio laughed. "Come, let's put them in the fryer." He carried the tray over to a huge pot of bubbling oil. Then he put the doughnuts into a metal basket which he carefully lowered into the oil. "Soon we shall have perfect doughnuts," he said rubbing his hands together. He smiled and his thick moustache rose like a fat caterpillar. But when he turned round, it dropped like a mossy stone.

"Hey!" he cried. "Stop!" All eyes followed Mr Fabrizio's. . . and this is what they saw: the big table was running red with strawberry jam. There was jam splodging from the table and puddles of jam on the floor. Yet more jam was squirting from the nozzle of the jam squirter, behind which stood Spider McDrew, his finger still on the button, his eyes on the woman making the gingerbread men.

"Stop!" cried Mr Fabrizio again.

"Spider!" shouted Mr Smithers. "Take your finger off the button!"

Finally Spider's mind slipped back into place. He released the button, noticing as he did the awful mess he'd made.

"Spider McDrew!" exclaimed Mrs Russell, her head wobbling like a jelly. "Whatever were you thinking of?"

"This is very bad," said Mr Fabrizio. "Very bad."

Spider's whole body drooped. He was so ashamed and embarrassed.

"I'm sorry," he mumbled. "I – I –" He wanted to explain to Mr Fabrizio about the gingerbread men – that they were his favourite cakes, that his mum made them at home and that he wanted to see if Mr Fabrizio's bakery made them the same way she did, so he could tell her all about the gingerbread men when he got home. But the words wouldn't come.

"You're a hopeless case, Spider McDrew," said Mr Smithers.

"I'm sorry," Spider said again. "I'll clear up the mess."

"Sure you will," said Mr Fabrizio. "Sure you will."

His face looked redder than ever. His moustache quivered with anger.

Spider was given a bucket of hot soapy water, a cloth and a mop.

"Now you clean that mess up good," said Mr Fabrizio.

"Yes, sir," said Spider miserably. He wished he could hide inside the bucket or put it on his head so that no one could see his flushed, unhappy face. He wished he'd never come to the bakery.

While Spider cleaned, Mr Fabrizio let the rest of the class make their own doughnuts. He stood them round a square table in the middle of the room and put a huge bowl of dough mixture before them.

"You take what you need," he said.

Darren Kelly decided he needed lots. His doughnut was twice the size of everyone else's. Hannah Stewart pointed this out to Mr Smithers.

"That is a bit big, Darren," said Mr Smithers.

"I got a big appetite, sir," Darren Kelly said.

"You could play football with that doughnut," said Jason Best.

"You could," Neil Phillips agreed.

"No, you can't," said Darren Kelly, "because I'm going to eat it." He rolled his eyes and rubbed his stomach.

When the doughnuts were done, the children carried them over to Mr Fabrizio to check. Then he pressed the button on the squirter and filled the middle of each with jam. Spider watched sadly. He had cleared up all the jammy mess and now he just stood to one side looking hot and sticky and forlorn.

At last all the doughnuts were ready to go in the fryer. Mr Fabrizio stroked his moustache and looked hard at Spider. Then he glanced at the big bowl of mixture.

"Mmm, I think there's a little bit of mixture left," he said. "It would be a shame to waste it." His eyes narrowed as they gazed at Spider. "You'd better go and make yourself a doughnut," he said. "But be quick."

For an instant Spider stared back at the baker as if he hadn't understood. Then his expression changed from bemused misery to pure delight.

"Thank you," he said. He moved and worked with unusual speed. He hadn't watched while the others were shown how to make their doughnuts. But it didn't matter. He knew what he was going to do. He had watched his mother often enough. Quickly his hands moulded and shaped the mixture until it was as he wanted it. Then, very carefully, he picked up the doughnut in both hands and carried it over to Mr Fabrizio.

Mr Fabrizio's eyes opened wide. His bushy eyebrows rose high on his forehead as he studied Spider's creation. It was not like the doughnuts the others had made. It was not simply a round, fat ball. Spider's doughnut had legs and arms, a head and a body, with a hollow where the tummy-button should have been.

"What is this?" asked Mr Fabrizio finally.

Spider beamed at the baker. "It's a doughnut man," he said proudly, "for my mum." The other children giggled and groaned.

"A doughnut man!" howled Kip Keen. "Spider's made a doughnut man!" He said it like this was the funniest joke he had ever heard.

"Spider *is* a doughnut man," said Jason Best.

"There's no such thing as a doughnut man," said Hannah Stewart crossly.

"Spider's made one, yeah, so there must be," Emma Flowers corrected her.

"Cra-azy!" cried Darren Kelly and he collapsed on to the floor.

"Now, that will do, class!" Mr Smithers

said loudly. Mrs Russell clapped her hands.

It took a minute or so to restore order. Some of the other bakers came over to see what was going on. They smiled when they saw Spider's doughnut. So did Mr Fabrizio. He smiled a round, friendly, doughy sort of smile. "I think it is excellent," he said. "Quite excellent." He squirted a big dollop of jam into the doughnut man's tummy-button. "A doughnut man for your mum." He shook his head and stroked his moustache. "Not a gingerbread man, but a doughnut man. Your mum is very lucky and you are a very clever boy, Spider." Mr Fabrizio's eyes sparkled. "Maybe *you* will be a master baker one day, eh?" he said.

Spider looked puzzled. He frowned at Mr Fabrizio as if the baker had asked him a very difficult question. Then he smiled.

"Why did the apple turn over?" he said.

Spider
and Geronimo

Throughout the summer term at Parkfield School the children had been doing work on the United States of America. They had read stories, learnt folk songs, drawn maps and pictures and discovered lots of interesting facts about the USA. The school's summer fair was to have an American theme, so the head teacher, Mrs Merridew, told the school one morning in assembly. The date of the fair was July 4th, which in America is a special holiday called Independence Day, she explained.

"This year we're going to celebrate it too," she said. "I'd like each class to do a little American presentation at the fair. Just something short – a dance or a song or a display of some kind. I'm sure you'll all have lots of good ideas." She looked around with a wide, confident smile. Then she sent everyone back to their classrooms.

Spider's class, as usual, were full of ideas. "We could have an American football competition," suggested Jason Best. He'd watched the American football Superbowl on television and replayed it later by himself in the garden, wearing his Manchester United football jersey and his bike helmet.

"Yes, cool!" Kip Keen agreed noisily. He stood up and hurled an imaginary ball through the air. Then he caught it himself and fell on to the table in front of him. "Touch down!" he squealed.

"I don't want to play American football," said Hannah Stewart. "Anyway, you need helmets and things for that."

"Hannah's right," said Mr Smithers.

"Any other suggestions?"

Emma Flowers put up her hand.

"Yes, Emma?" said Mr Smithers.

"What about square-dancing, yeah?" she said. "We could dress up as cowboys and do square-dancing."

"Yes, cowboys!" cried Darren Kelly. He made his hands into the shape of guns and started firing into the air.

"Thank you, that will do, Darren," said Mr Smithers. He smiled at Emma Flowers. "I think square-dancing is a very good idea. What do the rest of you think?" The question was met by a yip of approval. Emma Flowers looked as pleased as her guinea pig, Snuggles, after munching a particularly tasty carrot. But Neil Phillips had an objection.

"The girls can't be cowboys, because

they're girls not boys," he said.

"We can be cow*girls*," said Emma Flowers.

"Cowgirls, yes!" Hannah Stewart repeated and, swivelling in her seat, she pulled a rude face at Neil Phillips.

"That will do, Hannah," said Mr Smithers. "Cowgirls, cowboys, it really doesn't matter, you can be whatever you like."

A hand popped up in the air at the back of the class. Spider McDrew wanted to say something. He had been listening to the conversation with unusual attention. Now there was a look of deep concentration on his face.

"Yes, Spider?" said Mr Smithers.

Spider eyed his teacher keenly. He took a deep breath that turned into a wistful sigh.

"I'd like to be a cow," he said.

The class's response was immediate and explosive. Darren Kelly laughed so much he very nearly had an accident. Kip Keen put a finger up on each side of his head like horns and made mooing noises.

"Give me some milk, Spider," jeered Jason Best.

"That's enough," said Mr Smithers, staring hard at Jason Best and Kip Keen. Then he turned to Spider. "I'm afraid you'll have to be a cow*boy* this time, Spider," he said gently.

"Yes, sir," said Spider. "I– " But, not for the first time, Spider's tongue failed him.

He wanted to explain that the talk of cowboys had made him think of his special pet, Molly, his cow. Spider was picturing her standing in her field, chewing grass and enjoying the sunshine, and he thought how nice it would be to be a cow on a day like this. That's what he'd meant when he said he'd like to be a cow. He hadn't meant that he wanted to be a cow at the school fair. But, as usual, everything had got mixed up in his head and he'd said the wrong thing. He hung his head sadly and didn't say another word.

"You look a bit down in the dumps," said Spider's mum when Spider got home that afternoon. "Is something up?"

Spider told her what had happened at school.

"I'm always saying the wrong thing," he said gloomily.

"Come here," said Spider's mum and she gave Spider a big hug. Then she ran her hand through his spiky hair. "You're OK, Spider McDrew. You just do things differently, that's all. And good for you."

Spider smiled, then he frowned. "But aren't I a hopeless case?" he said.

"Oh, you're a hopeless case all right," said his mum. "And I wouldn't want you any other way. Except I wish now and then that you'd wear a pair of socks that matched."

Spider looked down at his feet. "Oh," he said. He was wearing one blue sock and one black sock with a picture of Donald

Duck on it. When he looked up again, his mum laughed and kissed him and Spider laughed too. Then a question buzzed into his head.

"Do cowboys wear socks?" he said.

Over the next week, Spider's class practised their square-dancing with the school's music teacher, Mrs Russell. She ran a country-dancing club after school and she knew all the steps. She had a special cassette of square-dancing music that she played while she taught the children how to 'do-si-do' and 'strip the willow'.

"Take your partners by the hand," she'd begin. Then she'd call out all the other instructions for the children to follow.

During the first few days there were a lot of hiccups. It was all a bit of a mess with children going to the right when they should have gone to the left or holding the wrong person's hand. Once Darren Kelly swung his partner, Zoë Cole, so hard that she lost her grip and flew across the room, crashing into the wall and ending up with her bottom in the caretaker's bucket.

Another time Neil Phillips tripped over Kip Keen's foot while doing a gallop and fell on Jack Smith, who walloped into Emma Flowers. The three children landed in a loud, squashed heap on the floor. Mrs Russell wobbled her head and sighed.

By the end of the week, though, the mishaps were few and far between. Indeed there was only one child in the whole class who couldn't get the dance steps right – Spider McDrew. He liked the music and he liked the dancing too. The problem was that he was always one step behind everyone else. When Mrs Russell called "strip the willow", he'd do-si-do and when she called "do-si-do" he'd gallop. Most of the time he ended up going in the opposite direction from his partner, Hannah Stewart, who got very cross.

"You're hopeless, Spider," she said and she complained to Mrs Russell.

"Spider, you really must concentrate," Mrs Russell told him. "You'll ruin our display."

"I'm sorry, Mrs Russell," said Spider. He looked meekly at the teacher. "I *am* trying."

"Well, you'll have to try a little harder," said Mrs Russell. "We've only got two days left. Perhaps you should practise at home."

"Yes, Mrs Russell," said Spider.

That evening Spider's mum got a real surprise when she came out of the kitchen to see Spider dancing up and down the hall, twisting and turning and making loud whooping noises.

"Whatever are you doing, Spider?" she asked.

"I'm stripping the willow," Spider panted.

"Skipping, you mean," said Spider's mum.

"No, stripping," said Spider, a little breathless from his efforts. "It's a cowboy dance."

Spider's mum laughed. "It looks more like a rain dance to me," she said. "Come and have your supper. There's a cowboy film on TV you can watch afterwards, if you like."

Spider's face lit up. "Thanks, Mum," he said.

Spider hadn't watched many cowboy films before. This one was very exciting. It was about soldier cowboys and the Chiricahua Apache. The name of the Apache chief was Geronimo. He had war paint on his face and looked very fierce. He didn't really want to fight, but the white men were trying to steal his land. They tried to make him go on to a reservation with some other Apaches, but he wouldn't. He tried to defend his home and won lots of battles against the soldiers. He didn't have many men, though, so in the end he made peace. But the head of the soldiers tricked him and didn't keep his promise to look after Geronimo and his people. So Geronimo ran away from the reservation and went back on the warpath again.

Spider liked Geronimo. He thought about him in bed that night and again the next morning. He was thinking about him at school when Mr Smithers called out the register.

"Spider McDrew," said Mr Smithers, studying his book.

"Geronimo," said Spider. Some of the children tittered. Mr Smithers looked up sternly.

"I don't see any *Geronimo* on my list," he said. "A simple 'yes' will do, thank you, Spider."

"Yes, sir, sorry, sir," said Spider. "I–" But he didn't say any more, because his mind wandered off to the cowboy film again. His head was full of gunshots and war cries – which didn't help his dancing when the class went into the hall later that day.

"Do-si-do!" called Mrs Russell. But

Spider thought she said "Geronimo" and he did a sort of war dance, running round on the spot, waving one arm in the air.

"Wa wa wa wa wa wa!" he yelped, patting his hand against his mouth. The rest of the class gaped at Spider as if they could not believe their eyes. Mrs Russell looked as though she were about to explode.

"Spider McDrew!" she shrieked, clapping her hands. "What are you doing?" Her face went very pink. Spider froze.

"I–I–I–" he stammered.

"You're a cowboy, not an Apache," Mrs Russell shouted crossly, her head twitching as though it were on a string. "And this is a dance, not a game. One more outburst like that and you are out of the display tomorrow. This is your last chance, do you understand?"

"Yes, Mrs Russell," said Spider miserably. His shoulders drooped and his hair flopped. He felt like a fool.

The rest of the practice passed in a kind of cloud for Spider. He did the steps as best he could and didn't make any terrible mistakes, but there was no life in his dancing. His heart just wasn't in it. Hannah Stewart 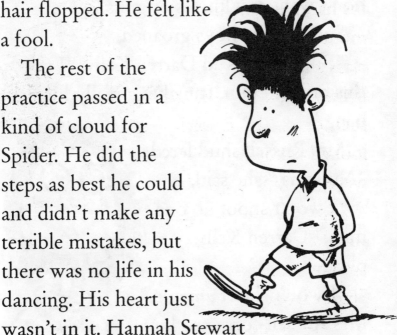 said her rag doll could dance better than Spider. Spider said nothing. He couldn't wait for the whole thing to be over.

"Right, children," said Mrs Russell at the end of the practice. "Now, I hope you all know what you're wearing tomorrow: checked shirts and jeans – that sort of thing. If you've got cowboy hats or neckerchiefs, please bring them. But we don't want any knives or guns."

Some of the boys groaned.

"But, miss," said Darren Kelly. "I got this brilliant gun. It makes a really huge bang."

Mrs Russell shuddered. "No guns," she said.

"I won't shoot no one, miss," Darren Kelly pleaded.

"I won't shoot *anyone*," Mrs Russell corrected him.

"No, nor me, miss," said Darren Kelly.

Mrs Russell sighed heavily and shook her head. "No guns," she repeated firmly.

"Can I wear my holster?" Darren Kelly persisted.

"Yes, Darren, you can wear your holster."

"And my sheriff's badge?"

"Yes, Darren, and your sheriff's badge."

"Thanks, miss," said Darren Kelly contentedly.

"Guns are stupid, anyway," said Hannah Stewart.

"OK, that will do for today," said Mrs Russell quickly. "I'll see you all at two o'clock tomorrow. And don't be late." She turned her gaze on Spider McDrew, who was staring down at the floor as though something very interesting was written there.

"Did you hear that, Spider?" she asked.

Spider peered up at her vaguely. His mind had wandered back to last night's cowboy film. He was thinking about a battle near the end in which the soldiers had shot lots of Apaches.

"No guns," he said solemnly.

Mrs Russell sighed. "At least you've taken *something* in today," she said. "Now off you all go."

When Spider got back from school he went to the field behind the house to see Molly, his cow. He stroked her nose and gazed into her deep brown eyes, as he often did. But, apart from saying "hello", he didn't speak. He sat on the gate and Molly stood beside him, bending down now and then to chomp some grass. It was a hot summer's day and the sun was still high and bright in the sky. Spider imagined that he was a Chiricahua Apache and Molly was a buffalo. Together they were roaming the prairie lands of the Wild West, looking for a place to hide from the white men and their guns: a place where the soldiers and the cowboys couldn't find them, a place where they could live in peace . . .

Spider was very quiet that evening and went to bed early. Next morning, when he woke up, he had made a decision. At breakfast he said, "Mum, I don't want to be a cowboy. I want to be an Apache."

"But, Spider," said his mum, "everyone's going to be a cowboy. You're doing cowboy dances."

"I know," Spider said. "But I don't like cowboys. I want to be an Apache." Then he told his mum about the film he'd watched on TV. "I'd really like to be Geronimo," he said.

"But what will you wear?" said Spider's mum.

"I don't know," said Spider, looking a little glum.

Spider's mum pursed her lips thoughtfully. "Why don't you look in the encyclopaedia?" she said. "There might be a picture there." So Spider looked up Geronimo in the set of encyclopaedias that were kept on a shelf in the sitting room.

There *was* a picture of Geronimo. But, to Spider's disappointment, it was a photograph taken when he was an old man, long after he had been captured by the soldiers. He looked very different from in the film. He still looked fierce, but he was dressed more like a white man. Spider read the section underneath the picture and learnt that Geronimo's real Apache name was Goyathlay, which means One Who Yawns.

"I want to be Geronimo like he was in the film," said Spider. "When he was a chief."

"Well, let's see," said Spider's mum. "You could get some feathers from the farm . . ."

Spider's eyes sparkled. "Yes," he said. "Great!"

So it was that, at one minute past two that afternoon, a small Apache Chief, complete with feather headdress and bright war paint, walked into the busy playground of Parkfield School and took his place among the cowboys and cowgirls. His entrance caused quite a stir.

A murmur of amusement and intrigue went through the crowd of parents and grandparents and aunts and uncles and children who were gathered to watch the square-dancing. No one had told them there was an Apache in the display.

But then, of course, nobody but Spider knew.

Mrs Russell gasped when she saw Spider. She waved her hand at him and wobbled her head, but for a few seconds she was quite unable to speak.

"Spider," she spluttered at last. "Spider." And that was all she could say. Mr Smithers came over and smiled.

"Well, you certainly know how to make an impression, Spider," he said, shaking his head.

"What a wonderful headdress!" exclaimed Mrs Merridew, who was waiting to introduce the dancing.

"You look brilliant," said Jack Smith.

"Yeah, cool," said Kip Keen. "I wish I'd come as an Indian."

"I'm not an Indian," Spider corrected him. "I'm Geronimo, Chief of the Chiricahua Apache. Geronimo means One Who Yawns."

"Cool!" enthused Kip Keen again.

Jason Best was not so impressed. "You're supposed to be a cowboy," he carped.

"Yes," said Hannah Stewart. "We're doing a cowboy dance, Spider. You can't be my partner dressed like that."

"It's OK, Hannah," said Mr Smithers,

"Zoë Cole isn't well, so you can dance with Darren."

"But what about Spider?" Darren Kelly asked.

Mr Smithers grinned. "Mrs Russell tells me that Spider does a rather good war dance," he said. "Perhaps you'd like to end the show with it, Spider, mmm?"

Spider blushed. "Oh, well, I–" he stuttered.

"Yeah, go on, Spider," Darren Kelly prompted. "Do that wild dance you did yesterday. That was really mad."

Spider's blush grew deeper, but with pleasure now.

"OK," he said. "It's not a war dance. It's a rain dance."

"Well, we could certainly do with some rain," said Mr Smithers. He looked up at the cloudless, sapphire-blue sky. "Just as long as it doesn't come until *after* the fair," he added. Spider beamed at his teacher with a smile that shone as brightly as the sun itself.

"Geronimo!" he said happily.

Spider's Birthday Outing

It was nearly Spider's birthday. He looked at the calendar in the kitchen and there it was, written in red felt-tip, "Spider's Birthday!" He counted the days and there were just seven to go – just one week.

"Mum," he said. "Can I have a party on my birthday?"

Spider's mum was washing up and Spider was drying. She rinsed the last plate and put it in the rack. Then she turned round and looked at Spider.

"Is that what you really want?" she asked.

Spider nodded so vigorously that his spiky hair flopped over his eyes.

"Yes," he said.

Spider's mum gave him a thoughtful look.

"The thing is," she said, "this house really isn't big enough for lots of children."

"We could go out in the field," said Spider brightly.

"But what if it rained?" said Spider's mum. She sighed. "Tell me who you'd like to invite."

Spider frowned. He frowned so hard that his face broke out in creases. Who did he want to invite? All of a sudden, his mind had gone blank.

"I don't know," he said at last.

Spider's mum shook her head. "You are a hopeless case, Spider McDrew," she said and she smiled. Spider dried the last plate and put it away in the cupboard.

"I've got an idea," said Spider's mum. "How about, instead of a party, we go on a special outing? We could go to the zoo or the cinema or a museum – and you could invite a few friends to come too. You know, just two

65

or three of your best friends. How about that?"

Spider's face was a happy glow. "Could we have a pizza?" he asked. He loved pizzas. In his room he had a leaflet from a pizza restaurant. He loved reading all the different names and thinking about which he would choose: Four Seasons, Savoury Sicilian, Country Feast, Hawaiian Supreme, Chef's Deluxe, Vesuvius, The Big One . . .

"Yes, of course," said his mum. "We could see a film and then go for a pizza if you like."

"Yes, please," said Spider.

"OK. That's decided then," said his mum. "Now *you* just need to decide who you want to invite."

It took Spider a long time to make his decision. It wasn't actually that difficult to decide, but his mind kept wandering on to other things – like what presents he might get, and the sort of pizza he'd order. By the end of the day, though, he had settled on three names: Jack Smith, Darren Kelly and Emma Flowers.

He sat down to write the invitations. He took great care over this, drawing a different picture on each one and putting down all the details in his best handwriting. To make sure he got the words right, he copied the party invitation he'd been given by Jack Smith, who'd had a birthday the month before. Spider made sure he put the right month on his invitation, though, and his own address and phone number; he wrote "outing", too, instead of "party". Then he folded the invitations neatly and put them into three envelopes, on which he wrote "Jack", "Darren" and "Emma".

Spider's mum came into the kitchen just as Spider was sticking down the envelope flaps.

"All finished?" she said.

Spider nodded.

"Sure you didn't miss anything out?" said his mum.

"Sure," said Spider.

"Date? Address? Phone number?" his mum persisted.

Spider smiled. "Yes," he said. "I put them all in."

Spider's mum ruffled Spider's hair.

"Just checking," she said. "I wouldn't want any disasters to ruin your birthday."

"No," Spider agreed. Then he wandered off into his own world again, thinking about his birthday and what fun it would be . . .

On Monday, at school, he handed out his invitations to Jack Smith, Darren Kelly and Emma Flowers. They tore open the envelopes and looked at their invitations: then they each smiled and said that they'd love to come.

"What sort of outing is it?" Jack Smith asked.

Spider told him.

"Hey, great! I love pizzas," said Darren Kelly.

"What film are we going to see?" asked Emma Flowers.

Spider frowned. "I don't know," he said.

"*The Great Kong*'s on at the Odeon, I think," said Jack Smith.

"*The Great Kong!* Yeah! I'd love to see that!" cried Darren Kelly.

"My big sister's seen it, yeah," said Emma Flowers. "She says it's really cool."

"Oh," said Spider. "Good." He didn't really care what film he went to see. He liked films, but he was more interested in the pizza he was going to eat afterwards.

"What film would you like to see?" Jack Smith asked.

Spider licked his lips and grinned. "The Big One," he said.

"The Big One?" Jack Smith queried. "What's that?"

"It's big and fat," said Spider, "with extra cheese and pineapple and sweetcorn and an egg on top." The others looked at each other and laughed.

"You're crazy, Spider," Darren Kelly said.

For Spider, the next few days snailed by. Each evening, after school, he ticked off another day on the calendar; he couldn't wait for the weekend to come and his special birthday outing. It was the only thing he could think about. In class, his mind wandered more than ever. Every time Mr Smithers asked him a question, Spider gave a totally wrong answer.

"What do you call it when birds fly away for the winter?" asked Mr Smithers.

"*The Great Kong*," said Spider.

The class giggled. Mr Smithers sighed. "Migration, Spider. It's called migration, not the *Great Kong*. Please pay attention."

"Yes, sir," said Spider. But try as he might, he couldn't concentrate. His thoughts kept flying away like birds migrating to another place, the warm and exciting place called "Spider's Birthday".

As it happened, someone else had a birthday that week: Neil Phillips. His birthday was the day before Spider's, on Friday. It was a custom that anyone who had a birthday could bring in one present to show the rest of the class. Neil Phillips brought in two new Subbuteo teams. One was Liverpool and the other was Tottenham Hotspur. His favourite was Liverpool, he said. His parents had given him a new football strip, too, but he didn't have enough room in his bag to bring it with him. Darren Kelly wanted to know all about it.

"You can see it tomorrow afternoon," Neil Phillips told him, "at my party."

"We could have a match," said Jason Best.

"Yeah, cool!" Kip Keen enthused.

"I'll bring my goalkeeper's gloves," said Jack Smith.

"But I don't like football," said Emma Flowers.

"You can be our fan," said Neil Phillips. He had only invited Emma Flowers to his party because his mum and Mrs Flowers  were best friends. He hadn't invited any other girls. He hadn't invited Spider either, but most of the other boys in the class were going.

At the back of the room, Spider McDrew stared forward with a deep and puzzled frown. This had nothing to do with the sums his teacher was now writing; Spider was thinking of what Neil Phillips had said about his birthday party. It was tomorrow, he had said, the same day as Spider's outing. But the really strange thing was that Jack Smith, Darren Kelly and Emma Flowers had talked as if they were going to Neil Phillips's party. But how could they go there, when they were coming on Spider's special outing? Spider was bemused. For the rest of the day, the question worried and nagged at him like an insect buzzing in his head.

At the end of the day, Spider walked out of school with Jack Smith.

"I'm really looking forward to tomorrow," he said.

"Yes," said Jack Smith. Then he stared at Spider. "Are you going then?" he asked.

Spider stared back at him in surprise. "Of course," he said.

"Oh, great," said Jack Smith, smiling. "Don't forget your football kit."

"My football kit?" said Spider and he looked blankly at Jack Smith as if his friend had been speaking another language.

"Yeah, we're going to have a match, remember?" said Jack Smith. Spider's blank expression turned to concern.

"But we're going to the cinema and then to have a pizza," he said.

Jack Smith grinned and shook his head. "Spider, you idiot," he said. "I'm talking about Neil's party, not yours. Your birthday's next Saturday."

"No, it isn't," said Spider. "It's tomorrow. Today's my birthday eve."

"It's not, it's next week," Jack Smith insisted. He put his hand inside his bag and pulled out Spider's invitation.

"See," he said. "Look. It says the fifteenth, like my birthday. That's not tomorrow, that's next Saturday."

"Oh," said Spider.

You are invited to an outing for Spiders birthday! On the 15th at 2o'clock RSVP spider

He stared hard at the invitation and what he'd written there. His throat tightened and his lip started to quiver as he realised what he had done. Jack Smith was right, it did say the fifteenth, the date of Jack's birthday. When Spider had copied Jack's invitation he had remembered to change the month, but not the day. He'd put the wrong date on the invitation. Looking at it now, he knew his birthday was ruined.

"Oh dear," said Jack Smith, who was almost as upset as Spider. He stood by his friend for a moment, as if waiting for Spider to say something. But Spider was too miserable to speak.

He remained as still as a statue, while all around children ran and shouted and said their goodbyes for the weekend.

"Do you want me to tell Emma and Darren?" said Jack Smith and Spider nodded sadly.

Spider didn't often cry, but he did that afternoon. As he walked back from school, his eyes were two waterfalls, pouring tears down his pale, sad face. When he arrived home, he threw himself sobbing into his mother's arms.

"Whatever's the matter?" she asked, amazed. Spider's sobbing grew even worse. It was so bad that, for a few minutes, he couldn't talk.

"I-I-I. . . th-th-th. . . M-m-my. . ." he stammered. Then he was overcome by another gush of tears.

"Oh dear, dear, dear. You poor lamb," soothed Spider's mum. "Just take your time. Don't hurry. Mum's here."

Finally Spider calmed down enough to tell his mum what had happened.

"Oh, Spider," she said gently, "you really are a hopeless case, aren't you? Fancy getting the date of your own birthday wrong." She stroked Spider's hair off his forehead and sighed. Spider's bottom lip started quivering again.

"I'm so stupid," he said miserably.

"No, you're not," said his mum. "You just made a mistake, that's all. Everyone makes mistakes."

"Not about their own birthday," Spider drizzled and he hid his face against his mum's body once more.

For a little while Spider and his mum stood in the hall together, he sobbing and she making soothing noises. When, eventually, he was a bit quieter, she led him into the sitting room and sat him down beside her on the sofa. She ran her hand through his spiky hair.

"What if we changed the day of your birthday outing from Saturday to Sunday?" she said suddenly. "Then you could have two special days." She smiled at Spider hopefully. But Spider wasn't convinced.

"But Sunday's not my birthday," he said mournfully. "I wanted to have my outing on my birthday to make it really special."

Spider's mum sighed. "Well, you just sit here quietly," she said. "I'll make some phone calls and see what I can do."

So Spider sat on the sofa, with his legs pulled up and his head slumped down, while his mum went out to the hall to the telephone. No sooner had she left the sitting room, though, than the phone rang. Spider heard his mum pick up the receiver and start to speak to someone,  but he was too deep in his misery to listen. All he could think about was his

81

ruined birthday. He didn't even look up when, a couple of minutes later, his mum came back into the sitting room. Her gaze fell on the unhappy huddle in the sofa and she shook her head.

"Spider," she called softly. "Spider."

Spider's sad eyes peeped up from behind his knees. His mum's face beamed back at him.

"That was Emma Flowers's mum," she said cheerily. "Emma wants to come to your outing tomorrow."

Spider's forehead wrinkled. "But she's going to Neil Phillips's party," he said.

"She'd rather come to yours," said Spider's mum. "Apparently it's a football party and she hates football."

"Oh," said Spider. He didn't quite know

what to make of this new development.

The phone rang again. Spider's mum went out to answer it. When she returned, her face was brimming with good news.

"Darren Kelly wants to come too," she said. "He says he'd rather see *The Great Kong* than play football and he's not that friendly with Neil Phillips anyway."

"Oh," said Spider, now totally dazed. He felt as though he were in a dream.

"Well, aren't you pleased?" said Spider's mum. "Your friends must like you an awful lot."

"Oh," said Spider once more. This time, though, there was a note of real pleasure in his voice, as he realised the situation: his outing was still on! Emma and Darren were coming. His birthday wasn't ruined after all. He raised his head and a joyful smile swept across his face. "Great!" he said. He sprang off the sofa into the air like a jet-powered frog. His mum laughed.

"Steady, Spider," she said.

But Spider couldn't be steady. He was so full of joy, he bounded about the room. Then he gave his mum a great big hug and a kiss.

"Thanks, Mum," he said. "You're the best mum in the whole world."

"It's your friends you should thank, not me," said his mum modestly. Spider grinned, but then, suddenly, his smile slipped.

"Jack Smith won't come," he sighed. "He loves football." Jack Smith played goalkeeper for the Parkfield football team.

"Well, *someone*'s coming, that's the important thing," said Spider's mum.

"Yes," Spider agreed. But he was still a bit sad about Jack Smith, because Jack was really his best friend. He'd invited Spider to his party. It had been the best party that Spider had ever been to. There had been a magician and a puppet show.

Spider was still thinking about Jack Smith's party when the phone rang for a third time.

"It's for you, Spider," said Spider's mum.

Spider gazed at her in amazement.

"For me?" he said. He never got phone calls, except from his gran.

"Yes," said his mum. Her eyes twinkled. "It's Jack Smith."

Spider's heart leapt. "Jack Smith!" he shouted and he raced out to the phone.

"Hi, Spider," said Jack Smith. "I'd like to come to your birthday outing, if it's on."

"It is," said Spider. "Emma and Darren are coming."

"Great," said Jack Smith.

"But what about Neil Phillips's party?" said Spider. "What about the football match?"

"I can play football any time," said Jack Smith.

"Anyway you're my real friend, not Neil Phillips." There was a short pause. "I'm really looking forward to seeing *The Great Kong*," Jack Smith continued.

"Yeah," said Spider. There was another pause.

"'Bye then," said Jack Smith. "See you tomorrow."

"'Bye," said Spider. He put down the receiver and then started bouncing about again. "This is my best birthday eve ever!" he cried happily.

Spider was so excited that it took him ages to get to sleep that night. But finally he did fall asleep and when he awoke the sun was shining on his birthday – and there was his mum with three presents to open. He got a smart silver cassette player with a couple of tapes, some chunky felt-tipped pens and a book called *The Indian in the Cupboard*.

A card came in the post from his gran with a five-pound note inside; and Spider even got a present from Molly, a big bar of chocolate! When he was dressed, he went down to the field to thank her. But he spent most of the morning up in his room, drawing with his new felt-tips and listening to a tape on his new cassette player. He couldn't wait for two o'clock, when his friends would arrive.

At last the front-door bell rang and there was Jack Smith, his friendly face pink and smiling. He pushed a card and a package at Spider.

"Happy birthday, Spider!" he said cheerily.

"Thanks," said Spider. He tore off the paper and there was another pack of felt-tipped pens and a pad with hundreds of different shapes on each page to colour in.

"You can make some brilliant patterns," said Jack Smith.

"Great," said Spider.

Darren Kelly brought him a packet of football stickers and a book to stick them into. Emma Flowers's present was a torch.

"Thanks," said Spider.

"It can shine red or green or white," said Emma Flowers. "If you put it on green, yeah, and hold it under your face like this, then you look like an alien."

"Hey, crazy!" Darren Kelly enthused. He took the torch and made his face go green. Then he turned the light to red.

"What do I look like now?" he asked.

"You look like a squashed tomato," Jack Smith said and the others laughed.

Spider's mum appeared. "Right. Cards and presents all opened?" she asked. Spider nodded. "Then it's outing time!"

The four children all adored *The Great Kong*. It was, they agreed, the best film they had ever seen. They talked about it all the way to the pizza restaurant and inside too. Well, three of them did; the fourth, Spider, joined in for a while, but the moment he sat down at the table in the restaurant, he fell silent. His eyes beheld the menu before him as though it were the most beautiful thing he had ever seen.

Soon the waiter came to take their order.

"Who's going to start?" said Spider's mum. "Emma?"

"I'd like an ordinary cheese-and-tomato pizza, please, yeah," said Emma Flowers.

"One regular," said the waiter, writing in his little book.

"Can I have a Hawaiian Supreme, please?" said Jack Smith.

"I want a Mighty Meaty," said Darren Kelly and he flicked his tongue from side to side like a snake.

"And what about you, Spider?" said Spider's mum. "What are you going to have?" Spider said nothing. He didn't even lift his head. There were so many different pizzas to choose from.

"I-I-I-" he stuttered. A picture wandered into his head

of the pizza leaflet in his bedroom at home. Suddenly he thought of something. To the surprise of the others, he stood up and pulled some sheets of folded paper from his back pocket. Sitting down again, he studied the crumpled sheets carefully, before handing one to each of his friends.

"What's this?" said Jack Smith, looking at the colourful picture of a pizza that Spider had given him.

"It's a card," said Spider happily.

"But Spider, it's your birthday not ours, yeah," said Emma Flowers. "You don't have to give *us* a card."

Spider shook his head. "They're not birthday cards, they're thank-you cards," he said. "They're to thank you for coming to my birthday outing. I did them this morning."

"Oh, that's nice, Spider," said Spider's mum.

The waiter coughed impatiently.

"And your order, sir?" he asked, tapping his pen on his pad.

Spider looked at him and grinned. "The Big Kong," he said happily. The others giggled. The waiter frowned.

"The Big Kong?" he said.

"He means the Big One," said Spider's mum. "Don't you, Spider?" Spider nodded so hard that his hair flew about like reeds in the wind.

"Ah, the special pizza," said the waiter, raising his eyebrows.

"Yes," said Spider's mum, "a special pizza for a special boy." She gave Spider a warm, glowing smile. Then she leant across and kissed him on the forehead.

"Happy birthday, Spider McDrew!" she said.